MY AFRICA VACATION

To my loving Father Chief Nwabuisi Iroaga, the greatest Dad ever!
Thanks for inspiring me to do my best in everything I put my mind to.
I miss you. You will be forever in my heart, I am happy that
Heaven has a new angel.

MY AFRICA VACATION

Written and Illustrated by Ozi Okaro

"Guess where I'm going on vacation this summer?" Arinze said to his friend Maddox.

"Florida?" said Maddox.

"No, Africa," said Arinze.

"Wow, that is cool!" Maddox said.

School had closed for the summer and Arinze and his family were excited about their trip to Africa.

"I am taking my favorite soccer ball," said Arinze.

"I am packing my new dress," said his sister Cheta.

"Make sure you don't forget anything because we will be very far from home," Mommy said.

The family had 7 suitcases in total, packed and ready for their trip.

Arinze was the first to wake up on the morning of the trip. "Wake up everyone!" He shouted. His loud voice woke the whole house up.

The Airport was very busy. They checked in their luggage and headed straight to the gate. "Wow, look at all of the planes," said Arinze.

"The large planes with two or more engines are used for international flights," Daddy said to him.

"Finally we are here," said Arinze, as the family landed in Nairobi, Kenya, their first stop in Africa.

"It's so hot, it feels like a sauna," said Mommy.

"Wow, look at the palm trees, just like Florida," said Cheta.

The van from the hotel at the Game Reserve had arrived and was ready to pick them up. "I love vans," said Cheta.

Early the next day, the family got ready for an exciting morning game drive. "I love going on safari," Arinze said as the family climbed into the truck.

"Let's see if we can spot the big five African animals," Daddy said.

"We are not even driving on the road," said Cheta. "Yes," said the tour guide, "this is the way to see the animals."

The next three days were full of spectacular views of animals and landscapes. "Look a Giraffe!" said Arinze. Cheta and Arinze spotted giraffes, elephants and a baby leopard resting with its mother.
On the last night in Kenya, Arinze said "time for our next adventure."

"What will we see here in Tanzania?" Arinze said. He was eager to know why the family had flown into Tanzania.

"I know," said Cheta, "we are going to climb Mount Kilimanjaro."

"Not exactly," said Mommy. "You are too young to climb the mountain so we are visiting the National Park surrounding it."

"This mountain is gigantic!" said Arinze.

MOUNT KILIMANJARO

Victoria Falls in Zambia was the next stop. "This is amazing, I wish Maddox could see this," said Arinze, "he would love it!"

In Egypt the Pyramids were breathtaking. "One day, I will figure out how they made these," said Arinze.

"I hope you do," said Cheta, "many people have tried."

"Oh I'm so happy we found a beach, this is my kind of vacation," said Arinze.

"Tunisia has some of the best beaches," said Mommy.

The family spent the whole day at the beach.

"Wow, I had no idea anything could be made of mud!" said Arinze, as the family observed Mali's Great Mosque of Djenne, the largest mud building in the world.

"I wonder what happens when it rains?" Cheta smirked.

It was a thrilling trip with one
exciting thing after another to see.
"The Senegambian Stone Circles
were made by a civilized society
a long time ago," said Daddy.

The family visited the Gold Coast called Ghana. "This area is historically known for its deposits of gold," said the guide. "Today we are visiting Cape Coast Castle, a fort where some Africans were kept before they were taken away on the European slave ships to America, Brazil and the Caribbean," he said.

In Benin, the family visited the 12 Royal Palaces of Abomey. "There is a long history of royalty and kingdoms on this great continent," said Daddy.

The visit to Africa would not be complete without a visit to Grandpa's house in his village in Nigeria. It was a pleasant surprise to see cousin Mezuo who was also visiting Nigeria for the holidays. Arinze and Mezuo got to play their favorite sport, soccer, also called football in Nigeria and many parts of the world.

"This is the best vacation ever," said Arinze.

It certainly was.

Also by Ozi Okaro . . .

DEPARTURES →

TRIP TO AFRICA

Written & Illustrated
by Ozi Okaro

ISBN: 0997131802
ISBN 13: 978 0 9971 3180 2
Library of Congress Control Number: 2016902981
Ozi Okaro Publishing
Montclair, New Jersey

Written & Illustrated by Ozi Okaro
Designed by Lawston Design

Made in United States
North Haven, CT
23 October 2022

25837202R00024